D0884185

With literacy and access for all

DUNCAN
AND THE
BIRD

DUNCAN
AND THE
BIRD

by Amanda Vesey

Carolrhoda Books, Inc./Minneapolis

For Jack

This edition published 1993 by Carolrhoda Books, Inc.

First published 1992 by HarperCollins, London
Copyright © 1992 by Amanda Vesey

All U.S. rights reserved. No part of this book may be
reproduced, stored in a retrieval system, or transmitted in
any form or by any means, electronic, mechanical, photo-
copying, recording, or otherwise, without the prior written
permission of Carolrhoda Books, Inc., except for the
inclusion of brief quotations in an acknowledged review.

Library of Congress Cataloging-in-Publication Data

Vesey, A.
  Duncan and the bird / Amanda Vesey.
  p.   cm.
  Summary: Duncan's attempts to feed the strange bird he
has hatched in his tree house lead to disaster when it
develops a taste for cake.
  ISBN 0-87614-785-6
  [1. Birds–Fiction. 2. Cake–Fiction.] I. Title.
PZ7.V6138Du   1993
[E]–dc20   92-37335
                              CIP
                              AC

Manufactured in the United States of America

1 2 3 4 5 6 98 97 96 95 94 93

High up in a tree, Duncan had a house.
    He never felt lonely in his tree house; he liked playing there all by himself.

One morning when Duncan went to his tree house, there was a surprise. On his bed, nestled in the blankets, was an egg.

It was a very large egg.

Duncan looked up large eggs in his bird book.

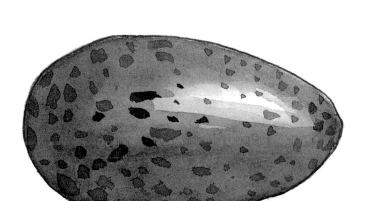

It wasn't the egg of an arctic loon.

Or a cassowary.

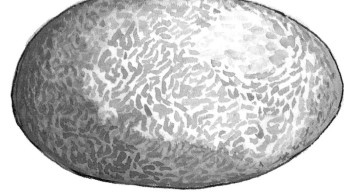

Or a king penguin.

The egg in Duncan's tree house wasn't at all like any of the large eggs in the bird book.

Duncan picked up the egg and shook it. Something inside the egg moved. Something inside the egg squawked.

   Duncan placed the egg carefully back in the blankets and watched it.

   He watched it all afternoon, until suppertime, but nothing happened.

The next morning, Duncan could hardly wait to get back to his tree house. He ran up the ladder and through the door.

The egg was gone.

His bed was all messy and crumpled, and when Duncan looked closer, he found large pieces of cracked eggshell in the blankets. There was more eggshell on the floor.

"Squawk!" said something behind him.

Sitting on the floor, behind the door, was a large baby bird. A bird with a green-and-yellow beak, black spiky feathers, and red webbed feet.

"Hello!" said Duncan. "What kind of bird are you?"

Duncan went back to the bird book.
  The bird wasn't a toco toucan—
they have colored beaks but
the wrong kind of feet.

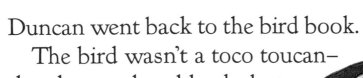

It wasn't a tufted puffin—
they have webbed feet but
a different kind of beak.

  It wasn't a hornbill or a pelican or a crane or a
blue-faced booby.
  The bird in Duncan's tree house wasn't like
any of the birds in the bird book.

"Where did you come from?" asked Duncan. He bent down to pat the bird's head, to show he was friendly.

Do you know what some birds do if you get too close? They peck you.

This bird pecked Duncan. It had a large beak, and it was a hard peck.

"You must be hungry," said Duncan. "I had better find you some food."

"Worms," thought Duncan. "Worms are what baby
birds like to eat." He dug around in the vegetable garden
until he found one. Then he carried it back to the bird.

"Here's a nice juicy worm," said Duncan.
"Open your beak and I'll pop it in."
    The bird inspected the worm.
    Then it stared at Duncan.
    Its beak stayed firmly shut.

"Caterpillars," thought Duncan. "Baby birds like to eat big, fat, hairy caterpillars."

He found a nice green one, munching a leaf.

The bird had its beak open and was
making a hungry cheeping noise.
Duncan dangled the caterpillar over
its open beak.

"Look, Bird," said Duncan,
"a delicious green crunchy
caterpillar. Eat it up."
The bird eyed the caterpillar.
Then it gazed at Duncan.

Its beak shut with a snap.

"You are a silly bird," said Duncan. "If you won't eat worms, and you won't eat caterpillars, what will you eat?"

The bird gave Duncan a look—a look that said, Would *you* eat worms and caterpillars?

Duncan thought he wouldn't.

"I'll have to try something else," said Duncan.

Duncan went home and raided the pantry. He put a can of baked beans, some cold fish sticks left over from the day before, a jar of peanut butter, and a piece of chocolate cake into a bag.

He took them back to the tree house.

"Baked beans?" offered Duncan. "Fish sticks? Peanut butter? It's delicious on toast."

The beak stayed firmly shut, but the bird stared hard at the chocolate cake.

"Cake!" said Duncan. "Let's try that." The beak opened very wide.

Duncan popped the cake into the bird's beak, and it disappeared at once. Not a crumb was left.

"That's what you like," said Duncan. "You're a cake-eating bird. I'll have to get more cake!"

Duncan spent all of his allowance on slightly stale cakes that he got for half price from the bakery.

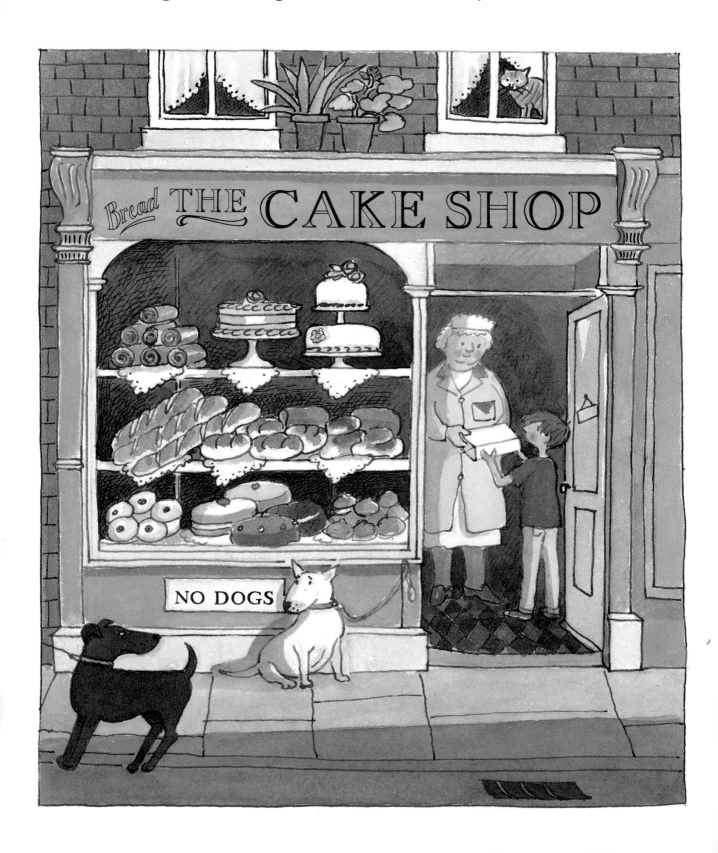

The bird grew and grew. It took up all of the bed, and it lay there most of the day, reading comics and waiting for its next meal.

Duncan liked the bird, but sometimes he wanted his tree house to himself. Wasn't this bird ever going to fly?

"It's time you learned to fly," said Duncan. He pushed the bird to the top of the ladder.

"Jump!" said Duncan.

The bird peered at the ground far below, then it stared at Duncan. Its feet stayed firmly on the ladder.

"Shut your eyes," said Duncan, "and try jumping off a little lower down."

Several times, the bird tried jumping from the lower rungs of the ladder. Each time, it landed with a thump on its flat webbed feet.

It became very hot and grumpy.

"Try again from the top," ordered Duncan. "And this time flap your wings hard when you jump."

The bird jumped. It flapped. Then just as Duncan thought there was bound to be a crash landing, the bird soared up into the air.

"You can fly!" called Duncan as the bird flew over the treetops and out of sight.

Over the river and around the town flew the bird. Over the church tower and the gas station and the school playground. Over some new houses and the dump and the biggest house in town—what was this?

The people at the big house were having a garden party. A wonderful lunch was spread out on long tables under a cedar tree.

"Oh, boy!" thought the bird, swooping down to the table. There were little cakes with pink frosting and cherries on top. There was chocolate-fudge cake and upside-down cake and walnut cake and Black Forest cake.

Gulp! The bird swallowed a whole walnut cake. Snap!
A plateful of cupcakes vanished down its throat. Munch!
Crunch! Champ! Chomp! Milk jugs flew, cups and
saucers twirled and spun.

The party broke up in total chaos.

"Mercy! Call the fire department!" cried the mayor, fainting into his wife's arms.

"By George, that's a fine-looking bird," barked the colonel. "I wish I had my gun."

"What's going on?" gasped Duncan. He was late for the party because his mother had made him change his clothes.

"A gigantic bird flew down and ate all the cake," they told him. "It was as big as an albatross and as black as a raven. You've never seen anything like it!"

Duncan thought he had.

"Anybody home?" called Duncan when he got back to the tree house.

There was no sign of the bird. On the table, melting slightly, was a wonderful ice-cream cake, topped with strawberries and meringues.

Somewhere, far above the trees, there was a distant, self-satisfied squawk.